Monkey Man

Takuji Ichikawa

An author who ignores traditional boundaries, and is impossible to pigeonhole. One whose positive and fantastical narratives touch the soul through storytelling that not only 'transforms and heals', but also sells in the millions.

Ichikawa, one of Japan's most creative authors with a completely unique perspective – even by Japanese standards – dreamt of becoming an author at primary school. He firmly believes in the transformative power of imagination; that dreams can come true, and that we can change the world we live in for the better.

After initially publishing stories on the Internet, his second novel *Be With You* became a blockbuster, selling more than a million copies in Japan, putting Ichikawa on the Japanese literary map.

The publication of *Be With You*, in fact, triggered its very own cycle of creativity by sparking the imagination of others, leading to the creation of a film and multiple international remakes, a television drama and a manga.

Ichikawa's works, which often depict love and loss, continue to resonate and be adapted for film both in Japan and further afield, and he continues to consistently demonstrate that literature should have no borders.

Translators: Lisa Lilley and Daniel Lilley

Lisa and Daniel Lilley met in Kyoto when they were studying Japanese language and literature. The impressive resilience they witnessed during the events of the Tohoku Earthquake inspired them to return to Japan after they completed their studies. They have now lived and worked together in Japan for nearly a decade, initially in Awaji and subsequently in Tokyo where they are now based.

Also by Takuji Ichikawa in English translation
Be With You
The Refugees' Daughter

A full publication list of all of Ichikawa's work is available from
www.redcircleauthors.com

Monkey Man

Takuji Ichikawa

Translated from the Japanese by
Lisa and Daniel Lilley

Red Circle

Published by Red Circle Authors Limited
First edition 2021
1 3 5 7 9 10 8 6 4 2

Red Circle Authors Limited
Second Floor, 168 Shoreditch High Street
London E1 6RA

www.redcircleauthors.com

Provisional Japanese title: モンキーマン

Design by Aiko Ishida, typesetting by Danny Lyle
Set in Adobe Caslon Pro

ISBN: 978-1-912864-12-6

A catalogue record of this book is available from the British Library.

*To my father, who was always tolerant,
and treated everyone with magnanimity*

Monkey Man

From the moment I first saw him I couldn't tear my eyes away. I couldn't get him out of my head. '*Why, though?*' I wondered. But I had no idea what the reason was. It wasn't that I *liked* him (at least I thought so, in the beginning). He just interested me.

He certainly was strange. Both his appearance and behaviour were so completely different from anyone else. That strangeness was what I first assumed might be the reason he had caught my attention. Those two traits alone – his looks and the way he moved – had a profound impact.

We met on the first morning after my transfer to my new high school. I was nearly late after getting lost on the way countless times. I was making a last minute dash towards the front gate when he came rushing out from the school grounds. I was sure we would collide. He hollered out, 'Hya!' His voice was high-pitched as if squeezed out from a rusty wind instrument. In an instant he shifted far off to my side and somehow avoided me. But, in doing so, he put himself in the path of an oncoming car. He shrieked again.

'*No!! You'll be run over!*' Just as I thought the worst was about to happen, he gently floated upwards, rolled across the car's windscreen and slid right over the roof.

The car braked to a sudden halt. A greying gentleman rushed out of the driver's seat. He looked around, his eyes spinning wildly. I did the same, also searching out the boy, but by the time we spotted him he had already run on ahead roughly 30 metres away from us. He waved in our direction and bellowed, 'Sorry about that!'

I stood there, stunned, watching him head off, when three well-built male students charged past me.

'Look, he's over there!'

'Stop! Don't you run off!'

The boy yelled out with another 'Hya!' Then, as if out of a manga, he jumped up with a *boing* and darted off like a rabbit. The trio of boys frantically chased after him but... Well, there was no way they could possibly catch up. His escape was far too quick.

That was the whole of it: my first encounter with Tengo. He made an incredible first impression.

From then onwards – because I was in the same class as him – I saw Tengo every day. I had plenty of time to observe him. The more I saw, the stranger he became. First of all, his body was terribly out of proportion. He was reasonably tall but incredibly thin and his limbs were unnaturally long. He wore clothes that weren't the correct size so he almost looked like an alien or some other creature failing in its attempt to imitate a human. He didn't seem particularly gifted academically and he was also hopeless at sports. (During football games in Phys. Ed. he was treated as *special*. A few times when the ball came his way he would miss so spectacularly that his shoe would fly off into a teammate's face. In a sense, he was a genius in his own blundering way.)

That was why our classmates made fun of him endlessly. The girls shunned him and the rougher boys treated him with incredible cruelty. That initial encounter on the first day of school was just one such example. It was as if his daily routine was to be chased around by violent boys from the sports teams.

'*Someone like him must always be alone, right?*' But that was not the case. He had two unobtrusive but eccentric companions who spent most of their time at his side. One of them was a petite boy with, for his age, a baby face. He almost resembled a primary school student. Thick black-framed glasses rested under his protruding forehead. Everyone called him Hideto. The other one was a tall and slender girl named Ran. When I first saw her I thought she was a male student. She kept her hair very short and wore a long black army coat that extended to her ankles. Always wearing chunky, tightly-laced boots, she dressed tough – like someone from a post-apocalyptic film.

Those three were always together in the school canteen at lunch. They sat at a table slightly removed from the other students where they enthusiastically exchanged words with one another. I tried glancing intermittently at them without being noticed, but it seemed my actions were obvious to Emi who was sitting across from me. I had become friends with her soon after I came to this school. We always ate lunch together in the same spot.

'You like him, don't you?' she said.

'What?' I huffed.

Emi deftly countered, 'Surely there's no way someone like Tengo could be your type? Right, Yuri?'

I was at a loss for words. Surely not… but not sure *enough* to actually say no. Why was I that interested in him?

'They're a really strange bunch,' Emi continued. 'Last autumn all three transferred to this school at the same time. Apparently they also live together.'

'Really? Are they siblings?'

'No, no, nothing like that. Do they even look alike at all? Their surnames are different, too. It seems they all live in some type of institution.'

'An institution?'

'Yeah. On the outskirts of town in the woods. When there's an issue with the parents or something, don't they take in kids like that? Not that I would really know.'

'Hmm, it sounds a bit complicated.'

'For sure. They're really closed off. They don't try to fit in with our class at all. In my opinion, they aren't the types I want to be friends with no matter what, so now I barely even notice them.'

In fact, everyone ignored them. They were ranked at the very bottom of the school hierarchy along with the geeky, insular model railway boys and the plain girls who had the presence of a waning midday crescent moon. They were the outsiders of our class.

The first time I exchanged words with Tengo the Outsider was about a month after my transfer. In the courtyard of the new high school there was a beautiful flower bed. It quickly became my favourite place by far. Was nobody else interested in flowers? Every time I visited not a soul was there. After school – as I sat on a bench by the flower bed by myself savouring the smell of the lilacs – Tengo suddenly burst into the courtyard in a frenzied state. He didn't notice me on the bench. Three boys from one of the sports clubs were chasing after him again. It looked just like a *Tom and Jerry* cartoon; routine, violent, comedic nonsense. Distracted by his pursuers, he stumbled over the bricks in the flower bed. With a thud, he tumbled to the ground. His trio of pursuers caught up quickly. They jeered as they rushed up to Tengo who was crawling on the ground and began assaulting him with their feet, laughing.

Instinctively, I rose from the bench and screamed with such a loud voice that I surprised even myself; a high-pitched sound like the whistle of a boiling kettle that echoed and reverberated around the bricks enclosing the courtyard. Everyone instantly focused on me. Their faces fell as if to say, '*This is bad*'. They must have thought no one was here. I was worried they would come over to me but instead they each muttered some throwaway comment and stomped out of the courtyard.

'Are you okay?'

As I rushed over he sat up abruptly, showing me a laughing smile.

'Thanks, you really saved me.' His face was scratched and blood was seeping out.

'Don't move, just stay still,' I told him and placed my hand on the wound on his face. He watched me silently. He had the most beautiful eyes; gentle, just like those of a giraffe. My face flushed. After about ten seconds I removed my hand from his cheek. I pulled a handkerchief out from my pocket and dabbed at his face where he was injured.

'It seems all right now. The bleeding has stopped.' I passed him the handkerchief and pointed to the dirty spots on his cheeks and chin. 'Tomorrow the scratches should be less noticeable.'

'Amazing,' he said, wiping away the mud on his face. 'Are you an angel?'

'Don't be silly. I'm just an ordinary 17-year-old girl. No white wings here.'

After I spoke, he started pretending to check my back for wings as if just to be sure. '*Was he serious?*' I laughed without realising.

'Anyway, are you sure nowhere else hurts? You got quite a kicking.'

'It's fine. There's a trick to it. I only hurt my face when I tripped. I had planned to fall better but there were buried bricks.'

I nodded that I understood. 'Somehow I sense that you let yourself get caught, didn't you?'

He stared back at me with deeply interested eyes and a slight grin.

'Why would you think that?'

'Why?... I just kind of know, somehow. I've had these types of unexplained feelings since about half a year ago... Either I have strangely good intuition or it must be, how do you put it, that the calibration of my "inner antenna" has gotten better.'

'Well, yes,' he said. 'I *did* get caught on purpose. Sometimes I need to allow them to let off some steam. Then they will leave me alone for a while.'

'So that's why you did it. Does that mean all that blundering about in PE was just acting, too?'

Conceding, he nodded. 'Hey, more importantly, the power that you just used to heal my wound – did it also appear around that same time as your intuitive powers?'

Now it was my turn to stare at him. 'How did you know?'

'I've seen it before. Kids like you, I mean. An *awakening* of sorts – a sudden calling. It reveals itself differently in each person.'

'Awakening?'

'Maybe it's a kind of adaptation? Because of the awful era we're in, yeah? An emergency switch somewhere in our genes, in our DNA, that gets turned on. Just like when a chrysalis grows wings, morphing into a butterfly.'

'Morphing into a butterfly... Hold on, are you saying *you* are the same, too?'

'No way,' he laughed. 'I'm just an ordinary 17-year-old boy. Ah, well maybe I am regressing a little and instead of wings I'm sporting a tail.'

7

'Really?' I said, as I pretended to peer at his bottom. He roared with laughter and shuffled backwards in retreat.

'I'm kidding. There's no way that's true.'

Like a spring-loaded doll he bounced up to his feet. He shook his body and flung the mud off his clothes in a way that really was truly primitive. Like a dog just out of water, he skilfully shook all the way up to his ears.

'Well then, see you.'

'What?'

With an abrupt spin of his heels he ran straight off. It was so sudden. I had no chance at all to stop him. Was he always like this? Unable to even stay still for a moment?

'Ah, my handkerchief...' I remembered too late he still had it. I considered chasing after him, but quickly gave up on that idea. I knew how fast he was when fleeing. Oh well. It was just a promotional gift I had received at the grand opening of a boutique (with the store logo in large print). *'I'll just let him keep it.'*

About a week after the incident in the courtyard, I was eating lunch with Emi in the canteen. As usual, I was looking over in the direction of the outsiders' table where I saw only Specs and the Army Coat Girl huddled together, chatting about something in hushed voices. Tengo had been missing since that morning.

'What's the matter? Worried Tengo isn't here?' Emi asked.

'Not particularly. Worried isn't the right way to put it. I just think it's unusual.'

'Happens a lot, actually. Doesn't he run around wherever and however he likes? Today is nice weather after all. He's like a dog unleashed.'

'Maybe.'

While talking with me, Emi was constantly using the mobile device in front of her.

When I asked, 'What's that?' she responded, 'It's a game called *Babel*. It's super popular right now.'

'Oh? Never heard of it.'

'Yuri, you really are clueless when it comes to things like this. What generation are you from, exactly? You're crazily old-fashioned, a total anachronism.'

'That's because in the town I used to live I was always surrounded by fields and mountains. That's how us country bumpkins spent our time, so we weren't plugged in to things like that.'

'You know, that's what makes you special, Yuri.'

'Thanks,' I replied quietly, a little embarrassed. 'So what kind of game is it?'

'To put it simply, it's a game that makes the world better. Teenagers all over the world are addicted. There're always millions of players connecting to *Babel*, all beavering away building a tower reaching up to the heavens.'

'Oh, so that's why it's called *Babel*...'

'Exactly. It really is amazing. I've never seen a game like it before. It's not about offence and attack power.'

Instead the players' weapons are love and kindness. You don't take, you give. Unique, right?'

'Yeah. But I don't really get it. In games usually defeating or robbing someone is what everyone enjoys, right? If that's the case, why's this game so popular?'

'I already told you, didn't I? It's only teenagers who are hooked. Generation Alpha. Older generations don't even give it a second glance. Purifying and regenerating a devastated, barren world is a scenario that fits us Alphas perfectly. Forming teams to kill and other such games are better left to old blokes who live in the world of Stone Age CPUs. Our generation is cooler and smarter than that.'

'I suppose so.'

'*Babel* is like a mirror world to the real one. Initially, the zone layout map was incredibly harsh. Heat waves and droughts, hurricanes, wildfires and tornadoes – not to mention pandemics and famine. And there are bonus levels including the complete line-up with exclusionism, war and everything that comes with dictatorship and tyranny. At the beginning everyone really suffered, but slowly everyone up-skilled and now things have started getting a lot better.'

'Up-skilled?'

'Yeah. At one point a boy gave some of his points to an opponent. Then 48 hours later – at least according to the in-game time – he realised his own points had increased by 20 per cent. Therefore, it's better to give to others, right? The slogan "No Give No Gain" suddenly started spreading and, after that, it quickly gained momentum.'

'What happens when your points increase?'

'Your status rises. And with a higher status you gain use of all sorts of abilities. Such as the ability to clean up polluted terrain, or the power to transform barren soil into lush, fertile farmland, for example. It's like having the ultimate "green fingers"! Oh, and then there's also the power to heal those hurt by pandemics or conflicts. In *Babel*, acquiring abilities like these is called "Evolution".'

Evolution... Could that have been the awakening Tengo spoke of...?

'What's wrong? You're pulling such a serious face.'

Surprised, I snapped back to reality hurriedly, shaking my head.

'No, it's nothing. Hey, besides that, what sort of people created this game?'

'Ooh, now that's a good question.' Emi learned forward dramatically and whispered into my ear, 'The truth is, this game was made by that group, Arlecchino. Surprised?'

'Arlecchino? The hacker group?'

'Yep. Apparently according to them, *Babel* is an important part of their mission. I suppose the idea of making the world a better place lines up with their goals quite a bit.'

Of course, it all makes sense now... Arlecchino. As Tengo had said before, we were living in an "awful era", and the hacker group was an organisation established to try to make things a bit better. Arlecchino took on mega-corporations, the military, politicians and The Complex that preyed on the world. Despite operating in different countries and under various names, the roots of The Complex were all interconnected. Spreading out underground, similar to a sticky, slimy, fungus-like mould, creating a vast network. Only a small part was ever visible at one time. Arlecchino exposed the connections. The Complex used manipulative language to sell completely unnecessary products to consumers that were actually nothing more than poison for the mind. The approach depended on the product, but zombified consumers are easy to manipulate further. The Complex wanted the domestication and the housebreaking of consumers. It was Arlecchino who showed us this. They revealed that what seemed initially to be naturally-occurring wildfires and such were actually caused by illegal deforestation, all conducted at the direction of The Complex.

To save the world it would take the combined actions of each and every one of us; that's what Arlecchino had put forward. The world was already at the brink. Whether we were facing a critical point or the point of saturation, I didn't know, but it felt like almost everything was about to erupt.

It wasn't just climate change and war. It had even reached the point where an unidentified virus was being named and cited as part of this strategic operation to search and destroy humanity. Infection rates were nearing 10 per cent of the population. In my town rates were somehow not that bad yet; but, after endless waves of different disasters, many countries and regions were imploding.

And yet The Complex wasn't trying to bring an end to these harmful activities that had continued for the last hundred years. They kept spewing out the sort of products that would all end up being toxic; always advocating for us to produce, grow, optimise the earth...

Only we could make it stop. If we changed our consumption patterns and eating habits as well as changing how we vote we could put a stop to the world's collapse. Arlecchino told us to 'be smarter'. To counter their destructive modus operandi, we needed to become accomplished experts working behind the scenes just as deftly – or maybe even more cleverly – than The Complex itself. We should be shrewd and cunning, pretend to be obedient but stick out our tongues in defiance behind their backs. We would never win without the same level of sophisticated deception. And *Babel*, no doubt, was the forum to learn this. Arlecchino knew the truth before any of us realised it, and were probably trying to casually and subtly inform us in the game. 'Evolution' could be one part of it. Surely they were aware of that. They were progressively waking up the planet's youth for something...

Suddenly the canteen became noisy. Everyone began intently peering at their mobile devices, excitedly raising their voices.

'What's this about?' Emi said, as her fingers slid over her device's screen. 'Oh, so that's it.'

'What?'

'Arlecchino have unmasked something, again. This time collusion between the government and companies polluting the environment. Apparently, they negotiated a backroom deal regarding the framework agreement on upper limits for CO_2 emissions. The environmental groups that received the information from them have published it on their websites. Have a look at this.'

Emi encouraged me to look at her screen. It showed a grainy monochrome video captured from a surveillance camera.

'This here, it's the CEO's office of the company that's been exposed.'

In the room a masked-man dressed completely in black was spray-painting graffiti on the room's walls: an hourglass inside a circle drawn using simple lines. Arlecchino, showing a united front, were displaying the mark of Extinction Rebellion. The mask fixed on the camera looked just like the face of Son Goku, *The Monkey King*, the character from the classical Beijing opera.

'Monkey Man…' I whispered.

Monkey Man was an Arlecchino operative. They utilised agents like him in collaboration with highly-skilled hackers. They installed backdoors using concealed malware created by the hackers to access systems at targeted companies. They'd done this sort of thing many times. Monkey Man was triumphantly showing off his physical prowess, which mirrored Son Goku. He moved almost as if gravity didn't exist. His outline had been spotted countless times scaling up the walls of buildings.

I looked up and glanced around. Everyone was pumping their fists into the air, screaming and yelling in delight. '*That's right,*' I thought. He was our rock star, the hero of Generation Alpha.

At the end of the school day, as usual, I dropped by the courtyard with the flower bed. Sitting at the bench was Tengo. His complexion looked awful.

'What happened today? Independent studies?'

'Hmmm… something like that. Because the sky was particularly blue.'

'That's your reason? Honestly, you do actually look a little bit ill.'

'I'm okay. Very fine, in fact. Even better than that…' He handed me a small white paper bag. I took it, and when I looked inside I saw a brand-new handkerchief.

'The handkerchief you gave me the other day, I washed it at home but the blood wouldn't come out. I tried searching for a replacement but they don't sell the same one, not anywhere. I guess it has a unique design. So this is a different one.'

Without thinking, I giggled. It sounded like he had gone to a lot of trouble.

'You really didn't need to go to all that effort. That old handkerchief was a promotional gift for the grand opening of some boutique. The design was the store's logo. It isn't sold anywhere so of course you couldn't find it.'

'Oh, so that's what it was! It was a real pain.'

I thanked him and put his gift into my bag. While leaning closer to examine his face and check on his injuries from the other day, I noticed the faint smell of blood. His cheek was completely healed. I quickly scanned the rest of his face but there were no injuries at all. I reached for his flank almost unconsciously. Just as I brushed it, he let out a screech, which sounded like a dolphin, and screwed up his body.

'Have you hurt yourself again?' As I asked he pulled an awkward-looking face.

'Just a little.'

'Was it those guys again?'

'No. But, similar types? Rough lots like them are everywhere.'

He was trying hard to hide the wound, but it was impossible. There was a rather large gauze dressing patching up his left side. It was seeping and blotted with blood. An injury like that would take some time to treat. Doing it there would have been a bad idea, as there was no knowing who might have shown up.

'Can you walk?' I asked, and he nodded, looking somewhat perplexed. 'Let's go. I'll prop you up.'

From the courtyard we moved to the Earth Sciences Preparation Room, which was hardly ever used. That was where I decided to tend to his injuries. I lined up three chairs and Tengo lay down across them. Kneeling on the floor next to the makeshift bed, I placed my hands on his side and on his chest. On his chest, I could see there were black and blue bruises from a beating.

'These injuries are awful… What happened?'

16

'It's no big deal. It's just that I totally enraged a bunch of nasty individuals and they were… really, really persistent.'

'This injury, it kind of smells burnt…'

'Really? I don't know why that would be.'

I glanced at his face. It looked as if he was telling the truth. I wanted to press for more, but I assumed asking wouldn't get me anywhere. So I didn't try.

'Yuri, your hands are warm,' he said after a while. Hearing him suddenly call me by my first name made me slightly lose my bearings.

'It's not only my hands. My body temperature is close to 38 degrees.'

'Is that also since half a year ago?'

'Yes. At first I thought I had caught some kind of illness. But then I slowly began to understand. Something, I think, was happening to my body.'

'An awakening.'

'Exactly. Arlecchino terms it "Evolution".'

'Oh?' Tengo said looking at me. 'You play *Babel*?'

'Not me. Emi told me about it,' I said, leaning towards his face. 'Is this a coincidence? Or rather, do you think Arlecchino knows something? About these awakened children you talked of?'

'I wonder,' he said and shrugged. 'There's no way I would know anything myself. But calling it a coincidence isn't giving them enough credit. Surely they must know something.'

Again, I had the sense that he had dodged the question. Tengo was always giving me that feeling.

'Hey, more importantly...' he said, 'what did it feel like? That's what I want to know. The time when you started your awakening, or evolution.'

'What did it feel like...?'

That's when I told him everything. About the rose-like rash that appeared at the start; the high temperature of over 40 degrees that continued for a week. I had initially thought it was a viral infection.

'The Misery Virus?' Tengo asked.

'Yes, that one.'

Society dubbed this new retrovirus The Misery Virus. Everyone it infected fell into a zombie-like state (in the sense of being a living corpse, not an immortal killing machine). The visible symptoms were always similar in everyone: apathy, amnesia, cognitive impairment and severe depression. Brain inflammation was said to be the cause, but many of those infected ended up taking their own lives before long. That's why the name, The Misery Virus, was coined.

But it was different for me. I didn't have apathy or melancholia. Rather, more than before, I felt as if my awareness was sharper and I could see things vividly, with greater clarity.

'And when did you notice your healing powers?'

'Fairly quickly. I have a younger brother. He suffers – like other children – from an autoimmune disorder and is very frail.'

Many children were afflicted with novel diseases in the early days. Maybe the polluted water and air were the cause, or maybe there were other reasons. Constant stress can cause the immune system to malfunction, or so some people say. But nobody really knew.

'One day my brother had a seizure, as he often did,' I continued. 'For some reason I tried putting my hands on his chest... Then the place I touched throbbed and became hotter, and his agitated, laboured breathing gradually began to calm down.'

'That was the first time?'

'Yes. When my brother had his next fit, for the first time I purposefully placed my hands on him and told myself that I could help.'

'An awakening. That's the moment you realised your ability!'

'That's right. It's strange but I felt as if I suddenly understood. Just like a baby's eagerly-awaited promised first words. When the right time came, I was simply able to do it without being taught by anyone... Eventually, as my reputation spread, all sorts of people came to me. I did as much as I could. Because so many were children they all somehow felt as if they were my younger brothers or sisters...'

'And your power treated those other people too?'

I nodded. 'To an extent that surprised even me. But shouldn't you know that?' And then I told him about the incident. A girl had suddenly collapsed in my old high school canteen. It had sent everyone into a furore. I had been sitting at another table at a slight distance with my friends. Someone had called the teacher who – upon seeing the state of her – immediately called an ambulance. As this was all taking place, the girl's condition steadily got worse and worse. The teacher frantically tried to save her and started rapidly administering emergency first aid. But the girl didn't react at all, she was completely still. Eventually the teacher's hands stopped moving. The girl had passed away… No words were uttered as such, but the expression on the teacher's face spoke volumes.

I had been completely overwrought with this all happening right in front of my eyes and that's when I managed to raise my voice for the first time. I said, 'I'll try,' as I squeezed my way through the crowd to the front. Everyone said it was hopeless, however I couldn't stop myself. I put my hands on the girl's chest but couldn't feel a heartbeat. It really seemed as if she had actually died.

Everyone was making a racket. Whatever I was doing couldn't possibly be called first aid; even so, I kept my hands on the girl's chest. One minute, two minutes, time kept ticking onwards. Eventually the sirens of an ambulance could be heard. The teacher thanked me, told me it was alright now and tried to prise me away from the girl. And then—

'All of a sudden the girl's breathing resumed. To be honest, even I was surprised. To have something like that happen…'

'Can you bring back the dead?'

'So it seems. That's what everyone was saying. They were as excited as if they had just been present at the resurrection of Lazarus.'

'Like a miracle…'

'It wasn't actually like that at all. I think the girl simply had extremely low blood pressure. So low her pulse couldn't be taken. They said she'd had an anaphylactic shock caused by food allergies.'

'Of course. But it was because of *your* power, Yuri, that she was brought back from that state.'

'Well, I suppose that's true… But that incident made me stand out far too much. From then on, things started to become difficult. The number of people coming, descending on me, increased multifold when compared with before. There were even patients close to death, in very serious conditions… On top of that, some kind of national research laboratory wanted to study my ability, or so they kept saying… They offered me an absurd amount of money. They were frighteningly persistent.'

'Did you refuse?'

'Of course. That's because—'

'Yeah, it's The Complex. I'm aware of other such cases. You were right to refuse.'

'I knew it… Anyway, because of all of that it was impossible to remain in that town any longer, so I moved here by myself. Now I live with an aunt from my mother's side of the family.'

'Hmm,' Tengo said. 'You're having a tough time.'

'It's not too bad. Aren't you also…?'

'Huh?'

'I heard you live apart from your family. With those two, your friends, in some sort of institution.'

'Ah, that's true. It's a long story. But it was my choice. It's fairly comfortable. You should come to visit sometime.'

'Is that really all right?'

'Of course. Because it's you, Yuri, you'd be more than welcome.'

'Oh. Well, maybe someday…'

Whilst we talked, I continued to keep my hands on him for around a further ten minutes, until his injuries were mostly healed enough that he wouldn't feel any more pain. He thanked me.

'It really is an amazing power. I understand why The Complex is so fascinated with it. Perhaps even Lazarus can be raised.'

'Of course not. I told you, didn't I? I'm just an ordinary 17-year-old girl. That kind of miracle is impossible. It's beyond me.'

'Ah, so you said. So, have you folded your wings up and taken a break from business?'

'Yes. Forever.'

From that day, Tengo and I quickly grew closer. By opening up and revealing to him the reason for my school transfer – a secret I had kept from everyone else – I felt

22

that what had seemed like a barrier between the two of us had come down. Well, just a little.

We usually talked with each other after school in the Earth Sciences Preparatory Room. There, we could spend time together unnoticed by anyone else.

'The house I lived in before coming here was deep in the countryside,' I said, while gently touching some minerals that had been arranged on a shelf. He was sitting on the floor, looking up at me as if dazzled.

'I was always running around by myself in the fields and mountains, with the plants and small animals as my playthings. Carefree, unconcerned about fashion, unrefined, ending up all covered in mud. Seeing me like that, my father would say I was just like *Mushi-mezuru Himegimi, The Princess who Loved Insects*. It really felt like that. I had no interest at all in things such as fashion magazines. After coming here, I've learned so much. Emi has told me about so many different things.'

'There's a coincidence. I am the same; I was born in a place absurdly deep in the countryside. It was a tiny settlement inside a mountain.'

'*In* a mountain?'

'Yeah. For generations my family line were its guardians. It was said the gods lived there because it was a sacred mountain. There was an uncut primeval forest of virgin beech trees that had been growing there continuously for eternity.'

'So your father was its protector?'

'No. My father was an outsider who drifted in from someplace else. Not long after I was born he wandered away again. Probably an incarnation of a mountain monkey. Well, that's what they said.'

'Really?'

'If that really were the case, I would be some sort of human-beast mix. Maybe that wouldn't be too bad though.'

'I'm not so sure…'

'My mother was very frail, so I was raised by my grandfather. He was ridiculously spartan. Even when I was only a child he took me on 10 or even 20 kilometre runs along precipitous mountain paths. Thanks to that, I got great training.'

'Just like that famous samurai, Ushiwakamaru. They say he was raised by a demon, a Great *Tengu*.'

'I suppose. Grandpa was also like a *Tengu*, or maybe a *Sennin* – a mountain shaman. He always said the weirdest things.'

'Like what?'

'For example, things like, "Souls dwell within the *Goshinboku* – the sacred *Yamazakura*, mountain-cherry trees. Our ancestors' memories are chiselled into their roots spreading deeply out through the ground". Or, "Should you go there you'll encounter your deceased forefathers and even the sound of their actual voices".'

'Did you ever hear them?'

'My ancestors' voices?'

'Yes.'

'Nope. Not at all, unfortunately. I'm still a disciple-in-training.'

'I feel like I can understand. That sort of makes sense.'

'Yeah?'

'When I was little, I often chatted with flowers and insects. My father told me about it. I only vaguely remember now, but somehow I feel like it really did happen.'

'That's the Princess who Loved Insects for you!'

'Yes. My father was right.'

'What else,' I asked, 'did your grandfather talk about?'

'Hmm… Oh yeah, he told me, "You have an important mission". He said that many times. "Mountain guardians are duty bound to protect nature. Your mission is to protect the plant spirits."'

'The spirits of plants?'

'It's called animism. Whether a mountain, a rock, a tree or a flower – spirits reside within everything. Grandpa said everything was precious, everything has soul.'

'That sounds difficult. There are so many things to protect.'

'Well, not really. At our mountain lots of golden-rayed lilies bloomed, and they said that within them reside the spirits of flowers. Yuri, I think you might be an incarnation of that very flower.'

'Me?'

'Yeah, you said so, didn't you? That you were a princess who could hear the voices of plants and flowers.'

'I suppose that was what I said. But if that's the case, are you saying you are my holy guardian?'

'Of course. I shall always be ready to rush to your aid no matter what, my Princess.'

I snorted involuntarily. It was a line that didn't suit him at all.

'I see,' I said, laughing. 'I'll totally rely on that. And if and when the time comes don't you forget!'

On another occasion, Tengo told me about the dog he kept in the mountains.

'A black haired shiba that Grandpa had raised. Incredibly smart, like a teacher born of the mountains.'

'So this time it's *The Jungle Book*? With the dog as your teacher?'

'I guess. Shiba dogs are similar to wolves, dignified and majestic. They're thought to be spontaneously independent. That's what they say, according to my grandfather. The leaders of all the beasts in the mountains. That's what they are.'

'Mountain beasts?'

'Wild boar, deer, monkeys. And even bears.'

'Bears? Aren't they dangerous?'

'Kunne was there, though. Oh, that was my dog's name. It's the Ainu word for black.'

'Even so…'

'Before, you said you conversed with plants and insects, right, Yuri? I think it was the same for me, that's how it felt. It was only in a vague imprecise way, but I believed I could communicate with the wild animals of the mountain. This was also something I learnt from Kunne. If you listen

26

carefully, then slowly you can kind of come to hear what they're thinking.'

'That's amazing! But it must be terribly difficult. It's a challenge to communicate even between humans.'

'Yeah. That's why I'm still in training. Eventually, if I can master it, I should be able to hear the voices of the dead.'

'Just like a *Sennin* mountain shaman.'

'Yes, that's my goal. Someday I'll be able to live off *kasumi*, the mist of the land.'

The first weekend after the rainy season started I was invited to Tengo's house. I was a little nervous, mostly because Specs and the Army Coat Girl would be there too. We hadn't even spoken together once. What kind of people were they?

The house – or was it an institution? – was on the outskirts of town in the woods. At first glance it looked more like the studio of a sculptor specialising in immensely large-scale art installations. It was a square, brick building with hardly any windows at all. I got a quick response from inside after I knocked on its large iron door.

'Hang on just a moment.'

Before long I heard the sound of the door unlocking. It opened and Tengo's face peeked out.

'Hey there, glad you could make it. Come on in.'

'I brought a little cake as a gift. For everyone,' I said, and passed him a box with a cake inside.

'Oh! Thank you. Ran will be pleased.'

'Is she here?'

'Yeah. Hideto as well. They've been waiting for you.'

I folded the umbrella I was holding and went inside. The impression upon seeing everything from the inside was that it really was like an enormous studio. It had high ceilings with exposed beams and duct pipes. There were lots of steel racks lined up along the walls with (and excuse me for being rude for saying so) what looked like junk with no clear function arranged everywhere in the narrow space. Where did they sleep, exactly? Some private hidden room on the opposite side of the back wall, perhaps? Somehow it didn't feel like a house where people actually lived.

There was a narrow space surrounded on three sides with racking. That's where Ran was. She was facing a line of monitors all in a row, tapping at a keyboard.

'Ran, Yuri bought us a cake.' Hearing Tengo's words, she glanced over, looked at me and mumbled something. Maybe it was a thank you, or perhaps a welcome, but it was spoken with such a low voice that it was impossible to discern. And then she quickly turned back in the direction of the monitors.

'Sorry, she's pretty antisocial. We're all sort of like that to a degree. If you had to coin a name for her it would be "The Princess Who Loved Binary Code". She was weaned on silicon chips. She loves software more than people.'

'What's she doing?'

'Who knows. It's her hobby; it's all Greek to me, completely incomprehensible. She's probably chatting with the spirits and ghosts in the electronic circuits about the futility of life.'

Encouraged by him, I moved deeper into the room in the direction of some finely upholstered sofas. Hideto was quietly sitting there. As we drew closer, his face rose up from his mobile device. 'Ya,' he said. Then, 'Welcome,' in a childishly high-pitched voice. Had his voice forgotten to break, perhaps?

'Good afternoon,' I said, sitting down facing him, my bottom sinking deep into the cushions. Somehow it seemed like an exorbitantly expensive sofa. Everything in this place felt wildly abnormal. What kind of place was it?

'So, this is the "institution" where you all live?' I asked Tengo, who was sitting next to me – but it was Hideto opposite us who answered.

'Yeah, that's basically it. It's a private institution. But, the truth is, it's run and operated by us.'

I looked at Hideto in surprise. Giving me a friendly smile he said, 'A group of minors living on their own creates all sorts of problems. So we hired adults and decided, for outward appearances, to call this place an institution. It's actually just the three of us, free-spirits, living here as we wish.'

'Is that true?' I turned to face Tengo and he nodded in agreement.

'The three of us met roughly one year ago. The country was holding a type of secret selection test. That's where we met.'

Suddenly a thought sprung to mind. 'Was it… the awakening you mentioned?'

'Yes, that's right,' Hideto answered. 'You have good intuition. That's another characteristic of awakened people. We were amongst the initial group of, let's call it, the doomsday-movement. About a year ago, the movement began to gradually spread almost like a fad amongst teenagers. However, the number of truly awakened people, in the real sense of the word, is still small. Commonalities are highly-advanced pattern recognition capabilities and intuition. And also a high regard for ethical standards and self-sacrifice—'

'Plus, each of us have our own unique individual abilities,' Tengo said. 'Yuri's, for example, is the power to heal.'

'Of course I tried to hide it, didn't I? But the truth was you were the same the whole time.' I glared at Tengo but he smirked and laughed, shrugging his shoulders.

'Everything is out in the open now! Though that makes things a little boring, doesn't it? The more mysteries a person has, the more interesting they appear.'

'Oh give me a break…' I said. 'Aside from that, your "unique abilities", what are they?'

'One look and it's easy to tell. I have enhanced physical abilities. After all, I am just like the samurai Ushiwakamaru, raised by the Great *Tengu*. As a result, I'm enriched with strength.'

'I guess mine is my general intellect,' Hideto said. 'I was already a member of MENSA. Even as an infant my

IQ was high. But if you compare then to now, before my awakening, I was probably just a regular science geek. A very boring kid.'

'And her?'

'Ran? She's generally good at computer stuff. She says her dream is to undergo cyborgisation, like Motoko Kusanagi from *Ghost in the Shell*, and plunge into cyberspace.'

'I don't really understand what you're on about, but you all sound like amazing individuals,' I said. 'Together, the three of you, what are you up to exactly?'

Tengo and Hideto silently looked at each other. Somehow there was a sudden awkward change in the atmosphere. What was going on?

Then, after a moment Tengo opened his mouth. 'Hideto said as much, yeah? Without any meddling from anyone, we just live here freely. For that reason this place is like our shelter, a sanctuary.'

'Of all the kids gathered in that place for the selection tests, the only truly awakened ones were the three of us,' Hideto said. 'We quickly realised it was a trap laid by The Complex, so we deliberately underperformed making our scores drop. That led them to promptly lose interest in us. Even now, selection tests are being held but it seems they aren't yielding any fruitful results. The truly awakened children – like us – hide their abilities.'

'In that place we understood each others' nature right away,' Tengo said. '"Ah! We have allies here!" We said as much.'

'Really?'

'Yeah. Awakened people sense it immediately. A fluctuation? A smell? It differs. But it was the same for you, right, Yuri? You noticed my existence.'

'That's—'

'You were intensely curious about me from the start. "Goodness, what kid is that over there giving off a wonderful aroma?" you thought.'

'What! Did I really seem like that?'

'It's just a metaphor. Or maybe not. Perhaps that's it word-for-word. Anyway, I knew, right away, that you were also one of us.'

'Ahhh…'

'Welcome,' Hideto said, 'to our very own "Institution for Gifted Youngsters".'

'Is that what you call this "shelter"?'

'That's right. It's a name loaded with magnificent satire.'

Contrary to first impressions, Hideto was "an adult male" and far more mature with an air of sophistication than his appearance and his age might suggest. He was also incredibly capable. Using a pseudonym, he had set up several businesses. He also had a number of electronics-related patents and ample capital. Apparently, he had used some of these funds to acquire their studio-like lodgings.

The two of them talked about themselves openly and rather frankly, but I still felt as if they were keeping something secret (or so my awakened intuition kept telling me).

Like Tengo, as I had expected, Hideto and Ran were also grappling with family issues which had lead to the three of them moving in and living together. Well, that's what they told me.

'My father was a professional *shogi* player,' Hideto said. 'He had a photographic memory that had captured records of the moves of a vast number of different matches from time immemorial. It was as if his head was stuffed full of them. He was the main figure in the last team of individuals to beat a computer opponent in an unofficial contest. He was as sharp as a pin but thoroughly lacking of any type of humanity. That was the problem. My mother's father – my grandfather – was a famous mathematician who rose as far as being nominated for the Fields Medal. Therefore, no doubt it was my father's intellect that attracted my mother. But she wasn't able to have the married life she had wished for.

'She had always been a naive and sensitive person but, after giving birth to me, her nerves got progressively worse, so much that sadly she now lives in a sanatorium. It's like the place that appears in the novel *Norwegian Wood*, where emotionally troubled people can live together in obscurity, avoiding all contact with the outside world. It is a temple-like refuge where women who have been scarred by abuse or rape can escape.'

'What? Does that mean your mother was also—?'

'I wonder. I never saw my father raise his hand to my mother but... I don't know. I think what injured my mother most, breaking her heart, was actually his complete indifference.'

'You must take after your mother.'

'So I like to think. I don't want to become like my father... but a ruthlessly calculating brain can also be a powerful weapon in this world. Because of that, even if there are such qualities residing inside me, I don't want to completely reject them. It's a complicated set of emotions...'

Ran was also a child carrying the burden of an unusual upbringing.

'Her mother was a famous actress,' Tengo said.

When I heard the name, I was surprised. She was a nationally renowned actress known by all. She had had the lead role, playing the heroine, in a romantic drama that even I had watched obsessively when I was much smaller. Her husband was also a well-recognised actor; the two of them were known for being a famously happy couple. I had thought their daughter was an actress as well. But when I said so, Hideto sympathetically shook his head.

'They were a happy family only in outward appearance. Their relationship had been breaking down for a long time. Ran's real father is actually the CEO of a certain IT company. He also already had a family. If they were found out, it would have turned into a major scandal. Ran's mother, before anyone around her had noticed that she was pregnant, took a long sabbatical, or what they call a "European Vacation". Ran was actually born in France. Afterwards, her mother's manager quietly brought her back to Japan, and her mother's sister adopted her.'

'Ran is pretty unconcerned and indifferent about it,' Tengo said. '"Just giving birth to me, that was sufficient," is all she has said about it. In that regard, at least it isn't something that she seems to be fixated on. But how she really feels, we don't know.'

'About the actress's daughter you mentioned, Yuri, that's her older sister from a different father. If you look closely, they actually resemble each other a lot. They both take after their mother.' Hideto stealthily glanced in the direction of the racking encasing Ran by the wall. 'That's why... Ran dresses the way she does. It's because she's aware of it and is trying to avoid any intrusive prying questions... Well, that's part of it.'

I wanted to leave their house before sun set. My aunt was very strict about the curfew she had set. When it was time to leave, Hideto let me know.

'We need to keep behaving the way we did around each other at school so it would be best for you to continue to keep your distance from us there. Try not to stand out too much. The Complex's fascination with the awakened is relentless. Because they're already aware of you, you can't be too careful. We'll leave all direct contact with you to Tengo – just him – as before. Pretend you don't know anything about the awakened. If anything happens

35

or you're in trouble let Tengo know immediately. Don't forget that we, your friends and allies, are here for you.'

I followed Hideto's instructions. I pretended not to know them at school. I only spoke with Tengo occasionally in the Earth Sciences Preparatory Room. My classmates wouldn't have had a clue about that. Only Emi with her keen observation (was she also one of the awakened, I wondered) suspected that something was going on between Tengo and me. But those suspicions were within the normal bounds of the imagination for a 17-year-old girl, and her guesses were limited to her gossipy interest in anything that seemed to entangle romance. And surely no one would think that the trio of unassuming outsiders, that no one paid attention to, at the bottom of the class social-hierarchy, were actually something close to awakened mutants?

'Look,' Emi said. 'The guy you're pining after is being tormented again.'

I looked over at their usual table where it seemed a boy from one of sports teams was trying to rub hair gel into Tengo's curly hair. A group of boys standing behind were cheering him on. Tengo was screaming and twisting his body around in an attempt to escape. Hideto and Ran ignored it all, continuing their conversation. Complete non-interference to the bitter end.

Once they had finished fashioning a magnificent pompadour-like quiff for Tengo, the boys left, sniggering amongst themselves. Tengo's face, which had been awkwardly distorted, abruptly snapped back to his regular straight face. When his eyes met mine he gave me a sly wink. It seemed the show was over. An impressive performance indeed.

Just like Hideto and Ran had said, awakened abilities could stay completely unnoticed and hidden if you laid low and continued to keep test results as unremarkable as possible. It was a form of camouflage. The three of them continued to live disguised as boringly ordinary students. What were they doing in the shadows, behind the scenes…? That was a mystery.

One day, after school, when I returned home my aunt said, 'A moment ago men claiming to be from some sort of research institute dropped by. They asked, "Is this Yuri's residence?" but I lied, saying I'd never heard of any child going by that name and sent them packing. They must have been the kind of people you warned me about?'

I nodded silently, and knew my face must have turned pale.

'They'll probably come again,' she said looking out of the window. 'They didn't seem to believe me at all. Maybe they checked the public residence records. What should we do?'

I shook my head. 'I'm not sure. I'll try asking my friends. One of them is very experienced with these sorts of things.'

'I see. Let me know as soon as you know what we need to do.'

'Okay…'

I went up to my room on the first floor and immediately took out my mobile device to dial Tengo. On the second ring he answered.

'What's wrong? It's rare for you to call.'

'They came to my house. The Complex. It seems we only just missed each other.'

'You're sure it was them?'

'Yes.'

'If they went to your home that's really bad. I'll come get you right away. Try to hide somewhere else.'

'Is it really necessary to go that far? Is it really that dangerous?'

'It's happened before. They're an impatient bunch. It's much better to be safe than sorry, really.'

'Understood. I'll be waiting for you.'

After I hung up, I immediately started packing. Hiding myself like he said would surely just be temporary, so for the time being I decided to put three days' worth of clothes into a small backpack. I also stuffed in some make-up and a copy of Yasunari Kawabata's *The Dancing Girl of Izu*, which was a reading assignment the school had given us. Was there anything else? As I continued deliberating and looking around the room, I heard something fall over with a thud downstairs. I almost let out an uncontrolled scream. I clamped a hand over my

38

mouth and listened intently. But I couldn't hear a thing. It was too quiet.

'Auntie…?'

The only reply I got was complete silence.

I opened my door carefully and went out into the corridor. As soon as I moved in the direction of the stairs and took my first step down, someone grabbed me from behind in a full nelson, restraining me. My mouth was smothered with a cloth that reeked of chemicals. Straight away, my vision started fading, and I then suddenly lost consciousness.

When I came to, I found myself in what looked like a white hospital room lying flat on a bed. I was wearing a white hospital gown; my midriff, arms and legs were fastened down with belts. Moving just my head, I turned to inspect the state of the room. It was about five square metres; windowless, with a stainless steel door visible in the corner of one wall. It looked just like an Intensive Care Unit in a television drama. Multi-coloured cords and tubes connected me to instruments that surrounded the bed.

Perhaps I was being monitored from somewhere? The door opened and a middle-aged woman in a white coat came into the room. She had metal-framed glasses and a bob-style haircut. She also had an extremely nervous look about her.

'I see you're awake. How are you feeling?' Without waiting for a reply she glanced at the numerical readings displayed on the devices, nodding slightly. 'There don't seem to be any problems. You'll be able to eat in just a bit.'

'Please let me go home,' I said. My voice was hoarse.

'That isn't possible at this stage,' the woman said. 'If only you had been obedient and cooperated with us, it wouldn't have come to this.'

'What about my aunt? What're you doing to her?'

'She's fine. Don't worry. A bit like you we just put her to sleep for a while. She should already be wide awake by now.'

'If that's true it'll mean she's out looking for me. She'll probably report it to the police.'

'Perhaps. But… that won't make a difference. No one will take it up or listen to her.'

I bit my bottom lip tightly. That might be true. The Complex was closely linked with all sorts of public bodies.

'If you cooperate obediently, your stay here will most likely become a comfortable one. We only want to understand your abilities. And put your power to use to help the world. If we can figure out how it works, how many people do you think we will be able to free from painful diseases? That's our objective. That's what we want you to understand.'

I didn't say anything. I fixed my eyes on the ceiling staring upwards and stoically suppressing my welling tears.

'Well, that's it for now,' she said. 'Full, proper examinations will start from tomorrow. I will show you your private room later. The restraining belts will be removed momentarily. They were just a precautionary measure. Sorry about that.'

She looked once more at the numbers displaying on the instruments, and then promptly left the room.

Just as the woman had said, shortly afterwards I was quickly untied and released from the bed. Two men in white gowns escorted me from the room. I saw a long corridor that appeared to continue without end. The walls and floor were white and lined with stainless steel doors spaced out at even intervals. There was no sign of any other people at all.

After a roughly 50-metre walk from the first room we reached the private room. It too was windowless. '*Maybe the site was a basement, deep underground,*' I thought to myself. I felt a claustrophobic-type of anxiety tightening up in my chest.

There was a bed placed up against one wall, as well as a simple white desk and chair combination. The far wall had a door (it was also white; it was hard to keep my eyes focused) that opened on to a shower room.

Standing started to feel difficult. I sat down on the bed. As I casually looked round the room, I noticed a book had been placed by the bedside. It was *The Dancing Girl of Izu*. Was this the only personal item that they had allowed me to keep? I idly turned the pages and thought about Tengo. 'I'll come to get you right away,' he'd said. Surely he must be very worried. I wanted to see him again. I wanted to touch his smiling face. I wanted him to tell me softly, 'It'll be all right'.

A single, isolated tear fell onto the pages of the book. I smothered my voice and cried. A crushing sense of helplessness filled my chest. Sobbing wretchedly, I cried myself into a state of complete exhaustion, and, before long, I fell into a deep sleep.

The examinations commenced the next day. They ranged from standard tests involving taking blood and urine samples, tests for electrical brain activity and electrocardiograms, as well as full-body cross-sectional tomographic imagery, to large scale investigations where enormous devices were deployed to thoroughly examine my insides in order to detect the most microscopic phenomena within me... Every possible kind of test imaginable was carried out continuously from morning to dusk without break. I was administered drugs by intravenous drip (and informed that it was irrelevant if I refused; if I resisted they could put me under and while I slept dissect me millimetre by millimetre). My brain was stimulated using magnetic irradiation and I was injected with various nutritional boosting supplements. I was constantly surrounded by more than ten doctors or researchers. The woman, from before, with the bob-style haircut, seemed to be the group's leader, and the others called her Director Saeki.

When the examinations were finished, I was completely exhausted and collapsed into bed, leaving the food that had been brought to my room entirely untouched. That became the routine. I was constantly tired and my body felt sluggishly heavy. To keep track of the days, I made marks on the back of the cover of *The Dancing Girl of Izu* using the handle of the wooden spoon they brought in at mealtimes. When those marks tallied six – meaning six days of confinement – the examinations entered a new phase.

The next stage involved a dreadfully old man. He must have been well over 100 years old. He was stretched out on a bed in the centre of the room, his vacant eyes staring up at the ceiling.

'I want you to heal him,' Director Saeki said.

'What kind of illness does he have?'

'All sorts of ailments. Widespread age-related genetic degradation—'

'If that was curable then no one would ever die of old age.'

'That's right. But isn't that the dream that humankind has been single-mindedly pursuing? That is this project's ultimate goal.'

I felt that at last I was starting to understand. Their ultimate goal was to fulfil the demands of the rulers at the top, the commanders-in-chief who reigned over The Complex. They wanted eternal life. This was something that rulers from all ages had desired. Even with the tremendous wealth and power they had attained, they couldn't simply slip in through the gates of Heaven. Is that what they found so mortifying?

'Who is he?'

'Someone who worked as the CEO of a certain corporation. It's said that its corporate affiliates number in the tens of thousands.'

So, within The Complex, this man was the top of the top; one of the individuals who had personally shaped the current world, with its one-to-a hundred million wealth gap. And, as if that in itself wasn't sufficient, now they were trying to create an emphatic lifespan gap, too.

'I can give it a try,' I said. 'Don't get your hopes up. To stop the progression of aging... I can't imagine it's possible to reverse the natural order like that.'

'Don't take such a defeatist attitude from the start,' she said with a slight sound of frustration in her voice. 'There's a possibility that your temperament may influence the results.'

I inclined my head and silently approached the geriatric man. Tubes and cords were connected to every part of his body. His face was etched with deep wrinkles. His eyes were open but his pupils were cloudy, making it unclear whether they could detect anything or not. Probably unaware of my presence, he simply continued staring up at the ceiling.

I put my hands on his chest. All of a sudden, I felt a sensation enter my fingertips. The hairs on my back stood upright. What was happening? It was the first time I'd felt anything like this. I squeezed my eyes tightly shut and focused all my attention on the tips of my fingers.

'What's wrong?' Director Saeki asked.

'No. It's nothing.'

My fingertips were still tingling. From the old man, some kind of horrible, stomach-churning negative energy was being transmitted. Maybe through the area I was touching I was sensing something from the dregs deep

44

inside his heart. Even if that was the case, *this* was the heart of a man who had reigned at the top of the world? Fear and anger. Miserable self-pity. Exaggerated vanity and superficial pride. It was like peering into the heart of an alpha monkey who had been ejected from the troop. Did that mean all those in authority who had clung onto their positions ultimately ended up possessing a mind like this? Regardless of whether they were a monkey or a human.

The negative energy was becoming a barrier. I couldn't keep my consciousness sufficiently concentrated. The figures displayed on the monitors tracking me began to reflect this.

'This doesn't seem to be going well,' Director Saeki said. 'That's enough for now. If we repeat this multiple times something will probably start changing.'

But things only got worse. I was thoroughly exposed to the geriatric man's negative vibes. I felt them so much that it hurt. Was this sixth sense-like sensitivity another example of the effects of awakening or evolution? Perhaps like a mirror neuron, which fires when actions are made or observed in others mirroring them, but with extraordinary specifications? Or was the truth that this old man was also awakened and this was how he, like other subjugators, used his power to crush other people's spirits in order to obtain their social status and positions? Somehow I thought that seemed more likely. These were the people who had gained control of the world with their dark abilities. Without these capabilities it would be completely impossible for one person to obtain such a huge proportion of the world's wealth.

The doctors kept administering new drugs to treat my exhaustion and lapsing powers of concentration. They were probably psychopharmacological drugs that acted as strong stimulants. I was constantly tormented by palpitations and tremors. I lost my appetite and my weight dropped rapidly. Even so, the testing continued. After all, I was nothing more than just a lab rat being tested to the limits, and once my breaking point had been reached a new one would be found – maybe that's all this was. I missed my hometown intensely. There was no green here. I felt as if I was suffocating. If only there was just one flower...

Day 13. Despite suffering from severe headaches caused by the psychopharmacological drugs, I was still managing to somehow continue to treat the geriatric man, when all of a sudden a device by the side of the bed started emitting an alarm. I was surprised to see that Director Saeki was trembling as she checked the numerical values displayed on the instruments. Around me, the doctors' movements quickly became frantic. As I stared at them in a daze, I felt something touch my finger abruptly. I looked up and the old man had grasped hold of my finger. His opaque eyes gazing toward me, he tried to say something.

'What?' I bent over and put my ear close to his mouth. But I couldn't hear any words. Only shallow breaths swept past my earlobes. He was so incredibly frail.

Once again I turned to face the old man. There were tears in his eyes. Immediately, I realised what he meant. Ah! *'You want to finally depart…'* The vibes he was transmitting through my finger were not like before and no longer felt so repulsive. His obsession over life and his fear of death had vanished completely. Now, his heart was completely calm.

Thank you… the old man's lips seemed to say as they moved. That was the end. I was hurriedly pulled away from the bed and swiftly removed from the room. I don't know what happened to the old man after that.

From that day onwards, my condition deteriorated even further. Day after day, I was too unfit to undertake any tests, which seemed to really frustrate Director Saeki and the doctors.

Maybe the end was near… *'Am I going to die here?'* I thought. I really didn't think they would allow me to return home. Contemplating the fate that awaited me made me feel as if my heart would burst with fear.

I wanted to see my mother and father. Even if it was just one more time, I wanted to hear their voices. I wanted to go back to that beloved home in my memories…

Day 17. I couldn't even get up from the bed. As I absent-mindedly stared up at the white ceiling, all alone, I heard someone's voice from just outside of the room. The door was closed. What was going on? I held my breath and focused my attention on the conversation.

'I got a telling off from above again...' The voice was muffled like an out of tune radio, but I immediately recognised the owner. It was Director Saeki.

'Is that so?' The other voice was definitely a male doctor I knew as Shindo. He was the Vice-Director.

'Yes... At this rate we'll never make any more progress. It's time we moved this to the next level.'

'You mean embedding electrodes?'

'Precisely. We'll have to proceed with preparations for cranial boring. I assume you've heard that a new type of implant has been developed? I would like to try that...'

'But there are still issues with it...'

'Issues? Isn't the real issue the situation that we find ourselves in right now? That implant is the solution.'

'I suppose so...'

That's when the voices cut off. For a moment I thought it was a hallucination, but the details felt too real. Had my hearing become abnormally sensitive? Or was it another aspect of the sixth sense thing? Surely this must be a further enhancement to the awakening phenomenon induced by my critical situation: the same as a rabbit's ears growing longer. The sensitivity of my inner antenna was getting increasingly better.

Yet it was horrible to think about it; a hole being opened in my head within which an implant with some type of 'issue' would be inserted. What kind of surgery was that? It was totally terrifying. I knew, in my state, it would be impossible to run away (in any case the door

48

was electronically locked, so I couldn't leave my room unaided).

I concealed my head under the blanket, completely alone and in isolation, and fought back against the encroaching fear. I couldn't stop shaking. On the verge of hyperventilating, I hurriedly took deep, calming breaths.

'Help me, Tengo...' Without meaning to the words tumbled out of my mouth. 'Help me, help me...' I was moved to tears, and my heart called out to him over and over.

'Please, save me Tengo...'

I was woken by chest pain. It seemed I had fallen asleep. I lowered the blanket down to my chest and took a deep breath. Unexpectedly, I thought I noticed a fragrance; the smell of flowers. I glanced to the side and there was Tengo.

'Hey, you awake?'

'This can't be real...' I mumbled doubtfully, still half asleep. 'I've been continuously calling for... Is this a dream? For you to be here...'

'It's not a dream. I told you, didn't I? I would be ever ready to rush to your aid, my Princess, in your time of need.'

'But... how...?'

He gently stroked my hair. 'I followed your black hair. My Princess is a Rapunzel at the top of a tower.'

'Top of a tower? Isn't this place underground?'

'Not at all. We are 72 storeys above ground. It's a skyscraper owned by The Complex.'

The surprise made me lose my voice, and then he offered me a single flower.

'I thought you must have been lonely without any flowers. I pinched it from the courtyard.'

'Ginger lily? It smells nice.'

'It's already withered a bit though. It's a long time since I picked it.'

'I still love it. Thank you.' I put the ginger lily flower into the pocket of my robe.

'I'm sorry it's taken me so long to come and get you,' he said. 'This room took a lot of time and effort to locate. And I had to be as careful as possible. I couldn't afford a single mistake. I knew if they got wind of it they might take your life…'

I nodded slightly. 'Even if that weren't the case, it was getting pretty close to the end… Those people, they were discussing drilling a hole in my head. They want to embed an appliance in me.'

'I see. That's why we hurried. Now, quickly, let's get out of here.'

'I… don't think I can walk any more. Also, that door is locked.'

Then it occurred to me. How had he entered this room? Just getting into this building alone must have been extremely difficult.

'It's all right. I have a key,' he said and showed me something small that resembled a matchbox. 'Hideto made it. A universal key. It can disable electronic locks.'

He reached behind his head, pulled out a mask and covered his face.

'That's—' It was the same mask I had seen on the surveillance camera: the face of Son Goku.

'Yeah, I am the Arlecchino operative they call the Monkey Man of Justice... Instead of wings I have a tail.'

'I knew it...' I mumbled. 'I had a hunch... and that means you lied again, doesn't it?'

'The element of surprise is the number one secret to popularity!' he said and shook his head a little. I giggled.

'What nonsense are you on about again?'

Carrying me on his back, he went to the door and unlocked it with his universal key. With a faint noise, the door opened. He popped his head into the corridor and checked the situation.

'It's just past three in the morning. None of the employees are here. Some security guards are on patrol but they aren't very attentive. And I put dummy images in the field of view of the surveillance cameras. This mask is just in case we run into a guard.'

Tengo's back was very warm. It made me feel strangely calm. My shelter. He ran down the empty corridor without making a sound. It was like flying through the air.

'You've lost a lot of weight,' he said. 'You've had a frightful time.'

'Yes, but that's already all forgotten. Because, Tengo, you came for me. Now I feel amazing.'

'That's good to hear.'

He seemed to know the structure of the building well. He chose passages without hesitation.

'You know your way around here very well. Way better than I do.'

'Hideto and Ran researched it. It was apparently really difficult for them, though.'

'Are they the brains behind Arlecchino?'

'Something like that. At the start it was just the three of us. A troop of boys and girls to reform the world. I think that's what awakening really means. We've been entrusted, called-on, by someone to save this planet.'

'Is that someone the Mountain Gods?'

'Maybe. And now, Yuri, you are one of us, too.'

'Is that so? I had no idea… Arlecchino? Me?'

'Yep. Ever since we first met.'

We were heading to the roof. Instead of an elevator, we ran up the emergency access stairs, climbing ten floors.

'Shouldn't we be going down?'

'That isn't possible anymore. The lower we go the tighter the security. Also, I broke in by climbing up the side and penetrating the building from the roof.'

'So, we're going to descend using the wall?' My chest hurt; it tightened with fear at the thought. Heights terrified me.

'Oh. But don't you worry. It'll be completely safe.'

I understood the meaning of his words as soon as we stepped out onto the roof. Tengo pointed over to a gondola designed for building maintenance, indicating that was what we would be using. It was a white rectangular box hanging from two wires extending from the tip of the arms of a mobile crane.

'It feels a bit like an amusement park ride. You can even watch the night sky at your leisure.'

He carried me onto the gondola, took out a mobile device and began tapping on its screen.

'This gondola is controlled from the central command room. That's why Ran hacked into it and we have control. I just sent a signal so it should begin to move in a moment.'

Before he'd even finished speaking, there was a blunt sound of a motor and the gondola began to shift. First, the long arm turned and the gondola pulled away from the edge of the roof. My body froze – paralysed. Under our feet, extending below, there was nothing but empty space for at least 400 metres. If the wires were to snap...

'It'll be fine,' Tengo said, then he squeezed my shoulder tightly. 'It may be better to sit on the floor. Then you'll only be able to see the sky.'

We sat down next to each other and waited for the gondola to reach the ground.

'Because it runs at seven metres per minute the journey to the ground will take less than an hour,' he said with a relaxed tone while removing his mask.

'That long?'

'Yeah, just like a Ferris wheel at an amusement park, the ride will take a while. Easily enough time for regular classmates to become lovers.'

My cheeks flushed hot and I looked down quietly. What was he going on about at a time like this? Not wanting to look flustered, I changed the topic.

'Hey, instead of that, tell me more about Arlecchino. I want to know more.'

Tengo nodded kindly, adjusting his position so he could sit facing me.

'Right, so about Arlecchino,' he said. 'It was all started by Hideto…'

Before his awakening, Hideto was already an extraordinary genius. He'd created the prototype for *Babel* when he was thirteen. After secretly buying up small game makers with the funds he reaped from several patents, he launched a project to commercialise *Babel*.

'He found an amazing group of individuals. Everyone was in their 20s. They were the generation who had grown up surrounded by Sony and Nintendo game consoles. Now they were rummaging around looking for a different path from the major game makers. They were very sensitive to the fact that game consoles could be used for something more than simple entertainment. That's why Hideto felt they were the perfect match.'

'That makes sense.'

'Yeah. Hideto was thinking about information dissemination and sharing. How can we make sure more of the young garner the information needed to begin building a truly sustainable world? That's where the idea of the game came from. In order to turn information and knowledge into wisdom, we need experienced-based awareness. And avatars used in gameplay generate a virtual experience. There's no better device.'

'So what you're saying is that by playing *Babel* children will realise how to save the world.'

'That's right. And after Hideto became awakened he further modified *Babel* to give it the added effect of encouraging the game's players to evolve. I don't understand the details, but if you are exposed to certain pulse frequencies – right here', he said pointing to his own forehead, 'the exposure turns on dormant DNA switches in our genomes. Like a disaster alert, perhaps. Look at the storm on the horizon. That kind of thing.'

'Then, slowly all children will become aware and have their eyes opened?'

'That's the hope. We can't just wait for the world to disintegrate, can we? According to Hideto there seems to be something like a threshold, a tipping-point. It's actually a rather surprisingly small figure. If only a few percentiles of all of humankind are truly awakened, then the world will start changing. They'll transform the value systems. Then, other people will follow these same values as a matter of course. The most important thing is changing the overall framework.'

'When you tell me things like this, I can only think that Hideto must really be a young genius.'

'Yeah, he's well informed and understands how people's minds work. That was true even when *Babel* was released. Hideto called on like-minded individuals who were also awakened to promote the game. "*Babel* is so crazily cool!" is what he got them all saying.'

Tengo listed the names of a few people: a famous Hollywood child actor, a world-ranking professional skateboarder, the youngest pop singer to ever win a Grammy Award, a charismatic young environmental activist…

'Even I know all those famous people! They're all awakened? Really?'

'That's right. I am not sure if it was that they originally had those qualities or being awakened gave them some type of advantage helping them excel, but it seems to be that amongst young celebrities and influential individuals there are many who are awakened. Thanks to them, *Babel* was a success. People are easily swayed by the eye-catching words of those with influence. That's the main principle of marketing, right?

'At the same time, in parallel, Hideto dedicated a huge amount of effort into exposing The Complex's awful actions and revealing them to the world. Not by exposing each individual act, but the age-old strategies employed by them that they keep out of sight behind the scenes. Like using repeated announcements that subtly permeate their messaging into people's consciousness.'

'And one operative assigned to that end is Monkey Man. That's you, isn't it?'

'Exactly. Kids like us who have been picked on; we all share that same desire to become heroes. Hideto calls it Peter Parker Syndrome.'

'But... Hideto is a child genius, and you have the physical abilities of a star Olympic athlete. Why were you bullied?'

'Ability has nothing to do with it. We were bullied because we were far too kind.'

Astonished, the realisation struck me hard in the chest, leaving me speechless. *Too kind.* That's the reason behind such maltreatment... What on earth *were* human beings?

'Hideto has been forever trying to dream up a new hero image, one that resembles him,' Tengo continued. 'A hero who is reforming the world through non-violent acts. Someone who, like him, has lots of money. Hideto was suspicious of Bruce Wayne, who poured everything into power suits and Batmobiles. Rather than waiting for wrongdoing and then punishing the criminal, money should be spent on prevention, or so he likes saying.'

'So that's why *Babel* has been exposing inside information on The Complex, right?'

'Yeah. He also set up a social media site and has done a wide variety of other things including launching a video streaming service. However, none of the people working there know that their boss is actually a 17-year-old boy.'

'A streaming service? He went that far?'

'Yep.' Tengo mentioned the name of a drama series. I'd heard of it. I had never watched it, but everyone in our class was always talking about it.

'In that drama, information that Arlecchino has secretly gathered on The Complex has been surreptitiously woven in. At first glance it's just a story about adolescent vampires, but by watching it kids come to learn about the true shape of the world. The audience figures have exceeded ten million. For a low budget drama from a start-up company, it's done pretty well. That's also another example of getting results by using our allies to promote it.'

Tengo's words stopped as he looked up to the eastern sky. Following his line of sight, I saw the black cloak of night had begun to show a slight blue tinge.

'Sunrise will be in about 30 minutes. It'll be the first time in a while that you have seen the sun, right?'

'Yes. Somehow it still doesn't feel real... Here, together with you, Tengo, welcoming in the dawn like this... I didn't think I would ever leave that building alive...'

'It must have been terrible...' Tengo gently touched my cheek. 'That lot, they only see awakened children as instruments for stuffing their pockets. They totally lack any shred of empathy. Even demons in hell show more mercy.'

'But why are they like that?'

'It must be an old instinct. Some notion of, "Wanting to stand at the top and lead others". Power and the very symbol of it, money, is their sole goal in life. It's also an old school human instinct to revere those types of people as leaders. Never stray far from the group. Obediently follow the boss's orders. Be wary of other flocks because they may be enemies that will harm you.'

'I think I know what you mean. The world is run on those three rules.'

'Yeah. But maybe, at least for the awakened youth, there's a chance to not be bound by those old traits? The newly updated brains of the new generation are far suppler. That's the constant battle between logic and instinct. Mass cravings and individual appetites, the aggressive impulses that are born out of self-preservation. If any of these are pushed to the extremes, they become toxic. By fanning those flames The Complex has magnified its wealth and power.'

'And as a result the world has ended up like this…'

'Right. They pollute not only the planet's oceans and its land but also the bodies and minds of consumers. But change is already afoot. The Complex is desperately trying to keep control of the market because kids are starting to notice their deceit. This was a trend that began with the Millennial generation. Unlike earlier generations, they didn't accept mass-market consumption. From that period, they were already more cooperative and less prejudiced. Perhaps around that time brains began their updating, who knows?'

'New brains seeking a new world?'

'That's right. The world is like a mirror, reflecting what's in our hearts and minds.'

Slowly, the sky began to colour a deep crimson red. Sunrise. I glanced down from the edge of the gondola. Surprisingly, there was a lush, green and hilly belt of land. Modern structures were clustered within rectangular strips of land carved out of the forest. Looking directly below us, there was a large river that seemed to coil its way around the tower. The only way to enter the building from the outside would have been to cross a bridge. It was just like a moat protecting a castle.

'It's a mini fortress. There's a network of sensors stretched all around the outside of the building. The only option is to cross the river but its current is very fast. It was really tough. The rain over the last few days also raised the water levels—'

Then and there, he suddenly stopped speaking and looked up at the roof of the building. The next instant, the gondola was rocked by a strong vibration, and then jerked to a halt.

'Look out!' Tengo laid down on the floor on top of me, covering me like a mantle. A muffled sound reverberated and I saw a bright red flash through my closed eyelids. *'What was that? That surging wave?'* I stealthily opened my eyes and saw that Tengo's face was distorted in agony. I knew instantly.

'Were you shot?' I asked, and he nodded silently. That flash must have been his pain resonating. The gondola began to move again, upwards.

'Our hack was discovered,' he said with some difficulty. 'They've taken back control...' Looking up, I saw about ten men with guns standing along the edge of the roof. I sat up to check Tengo's injuries.

'Stay down.'

'It's all right. They won't shoot me. It's not like we're armed. They are only trying to intimidate us.'

'That's pretty violent for intimidation.'

The bullet had pierced his right shoulder. I ripped the hem off my robe, wrapped it around his shoulder and then lightly pressed my hand over it. The bleeding was awful. At this rate his life would be in danger. When we arrived at the top what would they do to him? Would I get the chance to heal him properly? And in that case what would happen to me…?

'No,' Tengo said as if he could read my mind. 'Yuri, I'm not handing you over to those guys again.'

'But how can we—?'

'I'm trying to think of…'

Tengo carefully stood up and initially looked up at the guards on the roof. Then he scrutinised the ground below, turning his head to check the surrounding terrain. In the meantime the sky was slowly becoming lighter and lighter. Dawn was approaching.

'That over there,' Tengo muttered while casting a glance at the forest along the river. He sucked in his cheeks and let out a repeated short and sharp sound. It was high pitched like a bird whistle. As he did so, countless starlings flew out from the canopy of the forest and began to soar into the sky, fluttering around like a black tornado.

'This way it might be possible…'

He stared at me and said in a low whisper, 'Do you trust me?' I nodded silently. My mind had been certain from the start. Together with him…

He scooped me up and leaned out over the gondola's edge. My hair was blowing around in the driving wind. I closed my eyes and clung tightly to his neck. 'What are you going to do?'

'Ride the wind,' he said, hugging me close. Then, with great force, he dived off the edge. It all happened so fast; there wasn't even time to scream. When I opened my eyes to peek, I saw that the gondola was pulling away at a tremendous speed. It was as if my body was sliding sideways at great momentum. I heard the sound of several gunshots cutting through the rushing wind, but the bullets swerved harmlessly past us. It was strange, but I wasn't afraid at all. Falling together with Tengo, I felt I had acquired a strange, almost uplifting spiritual force.

Near my ear, I heard the sound of his whistle again. Almost instantaneously, the black tornado blew towards us, changing the trajectory of our fall from a perpendicular line to more of a parabola-like curve. A countless number of starlings gently bumped up against our bodies. A few seconds later, the two of us splashed down almost exactly in the middle of the river. The cloudy water was shockingly cold. As I sank deep down to the dark riverbed, I slowly lost consciousness.

When I came to, I was lying stretched out on a rocky shore. I sat up slowly and looked around. I saw Tengo collapsed face down on a rocky stretch about three metres away from me. I called out while crawling over to him.

'Tengo. Tengo?'

'Ah… yeah…' Tengo groaned in a low voice. Raising his head, he said, 'Where are we?'

'I don't know. It looks like we were washed far away downstream.'

'This isn't good, we're in plain sight… We'll be spotted by their search drones.'

'Let's escape into the forest. Can you walk?'

Tengo said he could and tried to stand, but he toppled over almost immediately. Fresh blood was seeping out from his wounded shoulder. How much blood had he lost?

'Don't push yourself too hard… Let's go slowly.' We helped each other along as we splashed and stumbled our way across the shore like amphibians walking on land for the first time. It took us five minutes to reach the forest's undergrowth only 20 metres away. I leant him up against the roots of a tree, re-bandaged his injuries once again and gently placed my hands on him. 'The bleeding isn't stopping. Without proper treatment…'

'That's impossible right now. Yuri, you need to do it…'

'But your wounds are deep. I'm not—' The wrinkled face of the geriatric man with his tears came into my mind. I wasn't able to save that person. What if that happened again…?

'Yuri, you can do it. Believe in yourself…' Tengo said, letting out a small clicking sound through a gap in his lips. What was that? I followed his line of sight and turned around slowly. To my surprise there was a doe standing right behind us. She was watching the two of us silently.

'A lookout…' Tengo said in a pained voice. 'Now the rest is up to you. I'm entrusting my life to you, Yuri.' After saying that, he lost consciousness again.

I was left alone. I felt helpless. A lonely shiver trembled through my chest. I turned to the deer standing behind me and our eyes met, as if she could hear me asking her for help. She stared right back at me. Her eyes were beautiful and showed not even a hint of fear. This was her realm after all. This was where the spirits of nature resided. The grass, the trees, the animals… If I could but borrow their power, then maybe…

I made up my mind and cuddled up next to Tengo's cold body. Death is cold; life is warm. I poured the warmth of my life into him. With all my body and soul I prayed I could heal his wounds. *'Please,'* I prayed to the invisible spirits. *'Please, somehow, save the life of the person I love…'*

It felt like I had been trying for quite some time. Despite intermittently losing consciousness, I kept going and never stopped praying. Tengo was in a deep comatose state. His warmth wasn't returning. His cheeks had turned blue, an ominous sign that death was silently creeping ever closer. What should I do? I had already tried and done everything I could. There was nothing left. But Tengo still wasn't waking up. The deep wound inflicted on him was beyond my healing abilities. If things stayed like this and he never came back… Just the thought made me feel sick with anxiety. What would it do to my heart?

There was a slight noise from behind me that sounded like a faint sigh. I turned around and saw the doe with the tip of her nose raised upwards, staring into space. Her eyes were pointing in the direction of a small camouflaged drone. They've finally found us! Security guards would be here very soon.

'Tengo, wake up!' He showed no reaction. 'Please, come back!'

My eyes welled up with tears. These people were callous. I had already abandoned the naive fantasy that I could possibly save Tengo. Ah. What should I do? How could I save him?

I felt the presence of something, and turned around. The doe had come very close. And it wasn't just her. Many other wild animals surrounded us. An impressive stag with magnificent horns, monkeys and wild boar, even a creature that looked a lot like a wolf. 'All of you… everyone is worried about Tengo, aren't you?' An animal, a baby monkey, leapt from a tree branch, knocking down the drone. The drone shattered on the ground and stopped moving. They were all trying to protect Tengo…

'Tengo, do you understand? Your friends are here. They're all worried about you. So please…'

I hugged his bone-cold shell of a body closely. I kissed his pale blue lips, and passionately breathed my life force into him with the warmth of my breath. *'Please, wake up…'* I was so overwhelmed I couldn't stop crying. I sobbed convulsively and kissed him again and again, countless times. A flood of tears streamed down to my lips and flowed into his mouth. Then, even though there had been no reaction before, slight changes in Tengo now began to appear. His Adam's apple twitched – ever so slightly moving up and down. He was trying to swallow my tears. His throat made a small cracking sound as a tiny quiver ran across his blood-drained eyelids. He was waking up!

'Tengo, Tengo!' I called out to him. He slowly began to open his eyes.

'Hey…' he said weakly. 'Is this Heaven? I can see an angel…'

'What are you on about? Even at a time like this…?' My voice was choked with tears. 'Look again carefully… I don't have any wings, do I?'

'That's true. That means the person here must be Rapunzel. You opened my eyes with your tears…'

'Oh, Tengo…'

'I have to wonder whether I am a vegan vampire who, instead of sucking blood, is revived by absorbing tears…?'

'It doesn't matter either way. I'm just happy that you came back.'

He nodded in agreement. 'Yuri, thank you… My life, its been saved because of you.'

'You really think so?' I murmured while untangling his hair. 'If that's true, it's because I wanted to heal you from the bottom of my heart. Love enhanced my power.'

'Love…?'

Suddenly, the wild animals started getting agitated. Surprised, we turned around. In no time at all, one of the guards carrying a gun had arrived and was right behind us. The baby monkey swung down, but the guard fired off a warning shot into the sky that roared and reverberated like thunder. The animals simultaneously darted off, fleeing deep into the forest. The guard came very close, stopped right next to us and glimpsed at the broken drone. He was a man in his mid-twenties and still had a young face.

'Are you carrying any weapons?' the guard asked Tengo.

'And if we were?' Tengo responded, the guard's facial expression changed. Thrusting out his gun he shouted. 'On the ground, face down!'

'What are you so scared of? Am I really so threatening, all roughed up in a state like this?'

'Shut up!' The guard struck Tengo's face with the tip of the gun's barrel.

'Stop it!' I screamed. He kicked me and forced Tengo onto his stomach, straddled him and this time hit his head with the butt of the gun. Tengo didn't resist at all.

'Stop it! He'll die!' I clung onto the guard's arm. He twisted violently to shake me off but I refused to let go. The longer I held on the closer our faces got. I felt all his fierce anger, rage and fear at once. It was the same as the old man. This young man was beginning to panic.

'It's all right,' I said without thinking. Those were the words that came out of my mouth. The young security guard stopped moving and gazed at me with a suspicious look.

'It's all right,' I repeated again and took his hand. It was an almost unconscious move. The power that had been dormant, sleeping inside me, sparked into life and my body began to follow a procedure of its own accord that it shouldn't even know. I closed my eyes and focused all my consciousness into my fingertips, which were touching the guard. Instead of weakening or forcing him to yield, if I could heal him, calm him… If I could do that…

After a short while, I slowly removed my fingers and opened my eyes. The young man was staring at me with a very confused expression. He stood up, retrieved the broken drone, then pressed the microphone switch on his collar.

'I've retrieved RP-12. They're not here. It seems they've escaped.'

As he turned to leave he looked at us one last time. His expression was strangely calm. It looked as if he might have given us a small nod but maybe that was simply a delusion. Either way, he was letting us go. It was his decision, made of his own free will. I hadn't forced him to do anything.

'That surprised me…' Tengo muttered in a raspy voice. 'I was wrong. It seems your power is limitless.'

'What do you mean?' I hugged him and put my hand on his bleeding forehead.

'The urge to attack is trouble,' Tengo said. 'It's some type of brain defect... a trigger. Things like hypo-glycaemia and inflammation, drugs, alcohol, or even tumours. They're all the same.'

'I see.'

'Many past dictators were the same... that's what they say. They were unable to control their primitive urges and instincts, fight or flight. Yuri, you have the power to return people back to their natural state.'

'I do?'

'Yes. That's what happened right now. You restored the mind of that security guard.'

'I was only... I just tried to ease his panic.'

'I think what you did, Yuri, was a much more funda-mental sort of healing. The restoration of reason. That power is the key to saving the world.'

'How so?'

'People all over the world are suffering from all sorts of cognitive malfunctions. They've lost the primary ability of reason and are easily swayed by anything that appeals to and cajoles their more primitive basic instincts.'

'Is that due to inflammation?'

'And other things. It's one type of delirium. Falling into a state of apathy and depression, or sometimes having that urge to attack brought on by uncontrollable panic. That's what The Complex wants and is trying to encourage, triggering these impulses with highly processed foods and additives, medicines, pesticides, different types of electronic devices and all sorts of things that utilise the narcotic known as convenience.'

'Really?'

'Yes. If we lose our reason to primitive instincts, the rest is simple. People will comply with whatever The Complex says. They'll dance along to their tunes of divisive rhetoric and see all other groups as enemies. Excessive collective group-demands generate a mandate for strong, autocratic aggressive and populist leaders. In short: dictators.'

'And that's why world is as it is now.'

'Yes, but whatever the case it's the awakening that's the greatest weapon for countering that lot.'

After that, it only took Hideto and Ran around 15 minutes to arrive to assist us.

'Sorry,' Ran said in a curt tone of voice. 'They caught on faster than expected.'

'It's no problem,' Tengo responded generously. 'It turned out all right. Mission accomplished. And Yuri treated my injuries.' Tengo told them the whole story from beginning to end.

'What a remarkable power...' Hideto looked at me, his eyes shining, after hearing the part about the security guard. 'Among our awakened friends, your ability really breaks the mould and stands above the rest. It's just what we were hoping for.'

'Really? I don't understand it well myself.'

'We, the human race, have been able to get this far and prosper all thanks to altruism. Kindness is the very reason why we didn't end up extinct and managed to keep surviving until today. If you look to the long-term future instead of chasing the short-term profits in front of your nose, you can see that cooperation is the only correct path forward. But brains that have lost their natural function don't understand this. Our minds have more or less been poisoned in the name of "civilisation". Humankind has lost its essential moral character.'

'Oh…'

'The Misery Virus as well. I don't think it exists in the way we are told. Certainly, if you were to run tests you'll detect a virus of sorts. But it isn't what is causing all this death. At most it causes mild levels of inflammation in the mucous membrane in the throat and nose.'

'Is that so?'

'It is. The truth is, the Misery Virus is used as a smoke screen to mask the poison dispensed by industry's numerous toxic products. The polluted brains and immune systems of consumers have fallen into such a dysfunctional state that they are led to apathy, depression and even suicide. It's hopelessness… that's the real misery – not a virus – causing despair and the deadly disease.'

'I'd no idea…'

'But we can stop this through awakening and healing. Your actions are the most important key to this. Yes… Your codename should be "Hope". Your existence is like a vaccine or a wonder drug countering the Misery Virus.'

'I am… Hope?'

'Yes,' Hideto said with a smile laughing. 'Not a bad name, right?'

To my surprise, the two of them had come by car. It was a fairly old pickup truck. Ran said she had driven.

'You have a licence?' I asked, and she showed me a card. It was flawless no matter how you looked at it.

'It's fake,' she said. 'Don't worry. Of course, I carefully created it from an original, doctoring the data. It'll hold up to any scrutiny.'

Naturally, Ran sat in the driver's seat on the way back.

'Now then, let's head off to the Institution for Gifted Youngsters!' Hideto shouted out in a childish, excited voice from the passenger seat.

'You said that before, but what exactly does that mean?'

'Well, what can I say. I suppose it's because our powers are like a gift from Heaven. Or something like that,' Tengo said from the seat next to me.

Hideto looked back and said, 'Evolution, or perhaps it's adaption, an upgrade needed for survival, right? To survive in this chaotic world we need to change.'

'Is that why we're the awakened?'

Hideto agreed with a big meaningful grin. 'But that's not all.'

'Huh? What do you mean?'

'A much more important level of evolutionary progress is occurring in the new generation. That's the gift from Heaven. You've seen it, it's right in front of your eyes.'

'I've seen it?' Then, without thinking, I glanced at Tengo sitting next to me. Shaking his shoulders, he imitated the hollering of a monkey, inviting me to laugh along with him. Perhaps it wasn't evolution after all, but regression?

'Do you understand?' Hideto asked. 'The ultimate evolution of intelligent creatures is the total forfeiture of the capacity to inflict harm.'

'The total forfeiture of the capacity to inflict harm...' It took me a moment to understand what he meant. Yes, that had to be it! That's the kind of aptitude the world needed right now.

'You may not have noticed but we've already entered that stage of development. It might be that latent DNA switches in our genomes have already been turned on, expressing new gene-related messaging.

'Are you following me?' Hideto asked, staring at me. 'Tengo didn't retaliate against those violent sports club members. He didn't return a single blow. We feel such a penetrating, adverse force compelling us against hurting anyone. It's simply intolerable for us to comprehend. This is caused by our advanced, highly-evolved mirror neurons. We've finally acquired the ability of restraint after being chased for so long. At last humankind is reaching the end of its childhood.'

I looked at Tengo again. He nodded as if to say 'Absolutely'. I saw Ran through the rear-view mirror. She also nodded. We're all the same. We can't hurt anyone. We're an evolved allegiance of friends.

Hideto continued, '*Babel* is, in a manner of speaking, a metaphor. In the game players gain increasingly more points the more they give away. The players reaching high scores that increase their status gradually lose their attack power. The attack power of a player who has reached the highest level is zero.'

'And that's just like the awakened youth,' I said.

'Yes. Kids that possess highly advanced mirror neurons will via innate mutual understanding and cooperation finally complete the Tower of Babel, no matter how confounding or malevolent a god stands in their way. That day is coming very soon.

'Think about it,' Hideto said, 'a world where the military no longer exists. If a person harms another member of their species, the human race, they'll feel vehemently and prohibitively conflicted. And, if all notions of violence and territoriality vanish from the world, then the current more than two trillion dollars of military spending could be used to keep climate change at bay, as well as to assist people who are struggling. And if this could happen every year? This isn't just a dream. We have the power to fashion such a world.'

Hideto paused, and looked at me with a smile and a laugh. 'You can't *not* get excited, just thinking about it?'

Afterword

This story is a companion piece to *The Refugees' Daughter* published by Red Circle in 2019, the fourth book in their series Red Circle Minis. The characters and narrative backgrounds differ, but both depict a similar world where 'boys and girls halt the collapse of the world'.

In *The Refugees' Daughter*, a girl wakes up to her special abilities in a world where billions of people have become refugees due to food shortages and conflict. The narrative follows the specific actions taken by girls and boys who have found their individual special abilities – *awakened* – as they struggle to find a way to halt the collapse of the world, and describes the concrete actions they take to achieve this. Both of these stories are long narrative tales condensed into short form, and there's no question that they feel fast-paced. I plan to develop a full-length version of this work that includes episodes I left unwritten. In regards to *The Refugees' Daughter*, I have developed a full version of about 250,000 Japanese characters in length. It was always the plan to publish these works in English first, in Europe and the United States, and to-date neither work has been published in Japan or Japanese.

The world is engulfed in crises of many different types; climate change, pandemics, wealth inequality, regional disputes and terrorism, and also the refugee crisis. How should writers like me deal with such things? In this era, what should a novel look like? My answer to that challenging question is narratives such as these; *Monkey Man* and *The Refugees' Daughter*, for example. They are tales of the voiceless, the weak and the oppressed, and those who have been distanced from public platforms by the power of dispute. These individuals don't use fists to punch people. They try to reach out to others, their neighbours, in a magnanimous manner that reflects the spirit and essence of maternal love: with tolerance, cooperation and non-violent acts.

I believe that narrative fiction has the power to change the world. One writer alone won't be able to generate a huge difference, but if there were ten, one hundred, or one thousand such writers, perhaps that will bring about change. I like to call this *Writers Without Borders*. If we build an inspirational network spanning the world maybe we can encourage voters and consumers to make the right decisions and elicit equitable action.

I was originally a romance novelist and a fantasy writer, and that influences how I write these stories, but I think each and every writer should pen a 'story to improve the world' in their own respective specialist genre.

A simple modest light, like this, can shine out on and illuminate our world, which today is replete with stories of violence, pessimism, punishment, misery and despair. I hope the day will come when these types of narrative tales, of love and kindness, brighten up our planet.

'The power of his storytelling is due to the candour of the feelings expressed. As if, confusing reality, somewhat magically, is what makes literature compelling giving it the power to delight and please.'

Le Monde

'*Monkey Man* offers us a glimmer of hope in a very dark, dystopian world.'

Alex Pearl author of *Sleeping with the Blackbirds* and *The Chair Man*

'It's a short, engaging sci-fi tale with a pointed message: the world's refugees are not a threat, a danger, or anything to fear – they are the hope for our collective future… Ichikawa's work is a masterful allegory that reminds us refugees are not our enemy; they are the future. They represent our best hope.'

PopMatters, **commenting on** *The Refugees' Daughter*

'I felt it in my heart, and it shook my soul.'

Kiyoshi Kodama, actor and former presenter of a popular Japanese television book review programme, commenting on *Be With You*

'In Takuji Ichikawa's high-concept *The Refugees' Daughter* (translated by Emily Balistrieri) a sixteen-year-old-girl and her family are trying to find an ominous "gate" to reach safety on the other side of a post-apocalyptic world.'

TLS, **commenting on** *The Refugees' Daughter*

'Reading this sent me into a trance. I discovered what love really is from this book.'

Ryoko Hirosue, Japanese actress best known outside Japan for her roles in *Departures* and *Wasabi*, commenting on *Love's Photographs*

Red Circle Minis

Original, Short and Compelling Reads

Red Circle Minis is a series of short captivating books by Japan's finest contemporary writers that brings the narratives and voices of Japan together as never before. Each book is a first edition written specifically for the series and is being published in English first.

The book covers in the series draw on traditional Japanese motifs and colours found in Japanese building, paper, garden and textile design. Everything, in fact, that is beautiful and refined, from kimonos to zen gardens and everything in between. The mark included on the covers incorporates the Japanese character *mame* meaning 'bean', a word that has many uses and connotations including all things miniature and adorable. The colour used on this cover is known as *Sumire-iro*.

 **Red Circle**

Showcasing Japan's Best Creative Writing

Red Circle Authors Limited is a specialist publishing company that publishes the works of a carefully selected and curated group of leading contemporary Japanese authors.

For more information on Red Circle, Japanese literature, and Red Circle authors, please visit:
www.redcircleauthors.com

Lightning Source UK Ltd.
Milton Keynes UK
UKHW011027140821
388796UK00002B/117